This book is presented to

TYLER

From _GRANDMA_

On _SEPTEMBER 30, 2009_

Because I love you
and there's no one like you!

Dear Grandma and Grandpaw Bear:

I know that if you would have known that grandchildren were this wonderful and this much fun, you would have had them first. The great thing about being a grandparent is that you can just love and enjoy your little grandcubs. And let's face it, at the end of the day, you can give 'em back!

The love that you give your grandcubs is a great gift. And it's a gift that will keep giving. The memories you've created and the love that you've instilled will be passed along to their children and to their grandchildren. Just think what you have started—a lasting legacy of love.

Whether your grandcubs are 3, 13, or 23, they're going to enjoy this keepsake book that will always remind them of the special relationship they have with you.

My Grandchild, There's No One Like You

Dr. Kevin Leman
& Kevin Leman II

Illustrated by
Kevin Leman II

Revell
a division of Baker Publishing Group
Grand Rapids, Michigan

Text © 2008 by Dr. Kevin Leman and Kevin A. Leman II
Illustrations © 2008 by Kevin A. Leman II

Published by Revell
a division of Baker Publishing Group
P.O. Box 6287, Grand Rapids, MI 49516-6287
www.revellbooks.com

Second printing, March 2009

Printed in the United States of America

Library of Congress Cataloging-in-Publication Data
Leman, Kevin.
    My grandchild, there's no one like you / Kevin Leman & Kevin Leman II ; illustrated by Kevin Leman II.
        p.   cm.
    Summary: When Belle and Bert Bear go to stay with their Grandbears, they all have a wonderful time.
    ISBN 978-0-8007-1890-9 (cloth)
    [1. Grandparents—Fiction. 2. Bears—Fiction.] I. Leman, Kevin II, ill. II. Title.
III. Title: My grandchild, there is no one like you.
PZ7.L537345Mxg 2008
[E]—dc22
                                                                    2008011127

Dedicated to the memory of my grandparents:

Grandma and Grandpa Leman

Grandma Buchheit

I cherish the legacy of love each of you left me.

Miss you.

"Is it time, Mama?" Belle asked. "We're all packed and ready."

Her brother Bert jumped up and down. "We're going to stay at Grandma's!"

Mama Bear checked her watch. "Okay, it's time to go."

That's all the cubs needed to hear. They grabbed their bags and ran to the car, singing, *"Heigh-ho, heigh-ho, to Grandma's house we go."*

There was nothing like a trip to the Grandbears!

elle and Bert burst through the front door of Grandma and Grandpaw Bear's den.

"We're here!" they shouted. And everybody hugged.

8

After a while, Mama Bear showed Grandma a list. "Here's what time the cubs go down for their nap, here are my phone numbers, here is the doctor's phone number in case of emergency, and—"

Grandma placed her paw on Mama's arm. "Oh, we'll be fine," she assured Mama. "You just go and enjoy yourself."

And with that, Mama Bear was gone.

Now we can party!" Grandma declared. "And what do we always do first?"

"Cookies!" the cubs cheered. And they all headed to the kitchen.

Grandma had the almond butter cookie dough all ready to go. Belle got out the cookie cutters while Bert helped himself to some dough.

"No one makes cookies like Grandma's cookies!" Bert said between licks.

As the next batch of cookies baked, Grandpaw came into the kitchen and sneaked a few off the cooling rack. Bert started to grab some too, but he stopped in his tracks.

"Grandpaw," Bert said, "why are you wearing your lucky fishing cap?"

Grandpaw grinned. Then he roared, "Because we're going fishing!"

Bert clapped his paws. "There's nothing like fishing in the lake!" he said.

The next thing Grandpaw knew, he got two huge bear hugs from Belle and Bert. And off they went.

It wasn't long before Belle and Bert brought their
fish to show Grandma. They were very proud.

But Grandma had something to show Belle
and Bert too!

Grandma had gathered together some old, dusty hat boxes and a big trunk full of funny clothes.

In no time at all Belle and Bert were dressed up in the old clothing. They put on a very fancy fashion show for their Grandbears.

"You know what that outfit needs, Belle?" Grandma said. She took off her most special pin, the one she always wore, and pinned it on Belle. "There. Now you look just like a princess!"

"Thank you, Grandma! There's nothing like your jewelry!"

"Oh, my goodness!" Grandma said. "According to Mama's list, we were supposed to have lunch two hours ago! We must have been having too much fun. Come on!"

They hurried to the kitchen table where a delicious lunch awaited them. Bert and Belle picked up their forks and were just about to dive into their green-bean-and-honey casserole when Grandma shouted, "Wait! At Grandma's house, dessert is first!"

Belle and Bert laughed. They turned to their dessert plates and dove into Grandma's award-winning Beary Very Berry and Banana Pie.

"Oh, Grandma," they said, their mouths full of berries, "there's nothing like your pie!"

Lunch was very tasty. Afterward, Grandpaw patted his belly and headed off to nap on the sofa.

"Hmm," Grandma said, looking at Mama's list, "according to this, it's nap time for you two."

Grandma let the cubs crawl into her bed, which was squishier than any bed they had ever slept in.

"You know what I think?" Grandma said. "I think I'd like to see which one of you can jump higher than I can."

And they all jumped and jumped until they were very tired.

"There," Grandma said. "After that, we all need a nap."

"No one does nap time quite like you, Grandma," Belle said. Bert stifled a yawn and nodded.

And the three bears curled up and took a nap together.

After nap time, Belle and Bert followed Grandma outside. They loved to help in her garden.

Belle found the most beautiful rose. "Look at this!"

"And look at this!" Bert shouted. He held out the slimiest snail.

"Well," Grandma said very quietly, "look at that!"

Way up in the tree was a bright red cardinal watching over a nest of eggs. Bert and Belle had never seen such a thing.

Belle sighed. "There's nothing like your garden, Grandma."

The day went by too quickly. The cubs were having so much fun. When they saw Grandma peering through her reading glasses at the list, they got a little worried. But not for long.

"I'm following Mama's instructions," Grandma said, "and we've covered almost everything. It says here that it's bedtime now." She winked. "But I think you need to stay up a little later. Let's make popcorn and watch cartoons!"

Belle and Bert helped Grandpaw pop corn in a great big pan on the stove. Only Grandpaw makes popcorn in a pan on the stove, and the grandcubs agreed there was nothing like that special popcorn.

Finally Belle and Bert could hardly keep their eyes open. Grandma read them a story and said a special prayer with them. Then she carried them to bed and thanked them for such a fun day.

"My sweet grandcubs," she said, "there's no one like you."

28

The years passed, and the cubs grew up. They never forgot their times with Grandma. They always remembered Grandma's special gifts, delicious food, and fun times.

But they knew that the greatest and best thing Grandma gave them was love.

A book for every cub in the forest!

Dr. Kevin Leman & Kevin Leman II

My Grandchild, There's No One Like You

Illustrated by Kevin Leman II

Dr. Kevin Leman & Kevin Leman II

My Firstborn, There's No One Like You

Dr. Kevin Leman & Kevin Leman II

My Youngest, There's No One Like You

Dr. Kevin Leman & Kevin Leman II

My Adopted Child, There's No One Like You

Illustrated by Kevin Leman II

Dr. Kevin Leman & Kevin Leman II

My Only Child, There's No One Like You

Illustrated by Kevin Leman II